EAR WORM

Ollie D. Hawkins

Copyright © 2023 Ollie D. Hawkins
All rights reserved.

For Lil Thrasher

(2017 - 2023)

Contents

The End 1

Shane 10

War 21

The Tub 34

Try Harder 42

The Tree 51

The Garden 59

The Blade 67

The Beginning 74

Ear Worms

Chapter 1

The End

I'm unsure whether it's the cold that keeps me numb or the gruesome reality that every last drop of blood has finally been drained out of my body. Either way, I don't care. The lack of any sort of feeling is keeping all the pain at bay. This small relief resulted in the happiest I have been in 6 years. Finally, it is all about to end.

FINALLY!

The gales at the top of The Rufus Blake Halls building are ferocious and show no signs of relenting. Initially, I imagined today would be the perfect day for it. Conditions at ground level felt ideal—no wind, no rain, with the added bonus that the sun appeared to have his hat on. However, by the time I entered the building and dragged myself up the 19 floors to the roof (which took the better part of 30 minutes due to my current health

Ear Worms

conditions, coupled with the broken lift; I swear, no lift in this country actually works!), I was once again reminded that God had other plans and decided to open the heavens for my big day.

Twat!

Of course, I should have guessed. When has a plan of my design ever played out in my favour in the last 6 years?

As I sit on the edge of the tower, gazing over at all the new beginnings of the students below me, I can't help but feel a simmering rage begin to rise up inside me. Why do they have the opportunity to live such a normal and happy life? What sin did I commit in a past life to curse me? Of course, I know the answer to that, but it's rhetorical. I had been a pretty good guy during my time (well… mostly).

I focus on the busy crowd below me and can just about make out the dirty outline of a decrepit homeless man, donning fingerless gloves and tracksuit joggers, blending from shades of

Ear Worms

brown to green to grey. He picks something from a wrapper out of the bin and begins to feed from it. Is this what I fought for? I imagine the state of that bin—the stench, cigarette ends, the worms, and maggots. How could a human put themselves in a position to live that way? It makes me feel sick. Everything here does. The hope and joy of the students. The sad old rough sleeper. Every single one of these members of the public is hopelessly unaware of the turmoil and troubles that men like me have suffered so they can merrily experience a "modern life". What Shane and I lost was much more primal—a sense of ourselves, or maybe who we are as a nation. Nobody down below cares. I don't care about them anymore either. That's a fair trade.

    As I glare at a young Asian student in glasses helping some old cow cross the road, I can't help but think about the bum feeding from the rubbish and the happy crowd below me. The

Ear Worms

rancour growing inside me feels like bile in my throat.

No wait…

That's just bile.

I empty the last dregs of my stomach onto the budding young academics below. No one notices, of course. My purge produces such little vomit that it would have dispersed quicker than the globules of rain now gushing. Still, I take great comfort in secretly defiling the unwitting victims. The crows pick at any matter remaining on the ledge. One small black eye of these feathery fiends twists away from my stomach contents sprawled on the ridge, having decided the dull pale flesh hanging from my bones is a tastier treat. The little bugger makes a beeline for my lower lip, and in one swift motion, tears the whole thing off my face, from corner to corner, revealing a reluctant permanent smile. Compared to my usual suffering, this new category of pain actually tickles. Somewhat takes the edge off. Despite cursing to

Ear Worms

anyone that would listen (a total of zero people), I can't help but find the mutilation of my face humorous as I flash a gory half grin.

"What the hell is happening?" I attempt to scream, but pronouncing any words is proving tricky with one lip missing.

Quick as a flash, I manage to catch the ambitious predator before he is able to fly off with his catch of the day. The crow squawks loudly and drops the worm, previously a part of my face, on the wet ground where I reclaim the flesh and place it firmly in my pocket.

What else could go wrong now? This whole ordeal over the past few days would have been laughable if it wasn't so traumatic. I absolutely can't take any more of this. What's next? I'm struck by lightning? No, that would be too good. Knowing my luck, I would slip back on my stomach contents and wake up in the safe hands of some good Samaritan. That would be my own

Ear Worms

personal hell on earth. No, I have to make this one work. I have to focus.

It's almost over. Not long.

I think of my mum. I don't know why; I haven't thought about her properly since the Falklands. She is such a saint. She didn't deserve a son like me, but I don't make up the rules. The man with the tattooed face does apparently. Then I think about dad, only because that's the way the mind works. I'm not actually thinking about him; his face just popped up.

I let my thoughts drift for a while longer, trying to think of other important parts of my life, but nothing of much significance comes to mind. Shane's face appears, but I don't see him. Not properly. Not how he used to look in life anyways. All I ever see now is the hole where his face was supposed to be. Even in old memories of school or the pub, he has no face—just brain matter and teeth shooting out of his forehead. Shane's mum pops into my head, and a whole new realm of guilt takes

Ear Worms

over my optimism of my situation. I recall the moment I was ejected out of his funeral by some wrestler-style cousins of his. She screamed at me, with mascara dripping down to her chin, shouting how it was all my fault. I know I deserved that, but it still cut me to the core.

    I thumb the weathered piece of dried derma in my pocket and realise how different it feels next to my soggy lip in the opposing pocket.

    When I eventually let my mind empty, a new feeling of adrenaline takes over. It feels so foreign, and I can tell my body is gearing itself up for the plummet. Dizziness begins to take hold, and I wonder if it's from the nerves or the various acts of mutilation I have recently committed on myself. I can feel that finally, my number has come up! I'm seconds away from plummeting to my death (finally my death!), and if I'm lucky, taking a couple of these hopeful young twats with me. Once again, a thought of Shane flashes through my mind, and I wonder if we will be together after this. Of

Ear Worms

course, I know there is nothing posthumously, but there is that one percent chance that at least one of these absurd religions is actually correct in their faith in a higher being. But what am I expecting? To visit Saint Peter at those pearly gates, with a big smile and open arms as he exclaims, "Come right through mate, we got birds on tap in here!"? If there is an afterlife, I won't be visiting anytime soon; that is for certain. No, I am destined for the eternal inferno. The best I can hope for is sweet nothingness. Just black. Endless darkness. What a treat that will be after my years of suffering. No more guilt, shame, or PTSD. Just black.

Shane's up here, stood next to me. I can smell that awful putrid smell. My final image of him. That's the only way I ever get to see him now —in this grim, ghostly hallucination that will haunt me until my last day (last day? That's today!)

What am I waiting for? I am completely adamant that this is it. I can feel it in the core of my stomach. That one experience at the roulette table

Ear Worms

springs to mind again, but more definite than that time, and I am comforted by this knowledge. Of course, I have had this feeling before. But this time it is different. This time it's not just pure impulse guiding me, but also logic. It is actually impossible for me to survive, with or without this curse hanging over me. This really is finally about to happen.

The end! My end! Everything ends.
Finally.
I smile as I push myself off the ledge and see the pavement rushing towards me.

Ear Worms
Chapter 2
Shane

There is that tired old cliché that your life supposedly flashes before your eyes when you die. I can categorically tell you that is another bare-faced lie we are consistently told throughout our lives. There is no peace. We don't find inner truth or any sort of meaning to any of it. However, something interesting did happen to me in my final seconds on this earth. A poignant scene from my past found its way into my consciousness. This was the pivotal moment I chose to ruin both of our lives. The last time before we crossed the Rubicon. Of course, this final image in my mind before my eventual demise was of Shane.

    My thoughts decide to take me back to one of the many debauched nights we shared. I recall this event in the same way I remember his face. The evening in question sort of blurs into one murky, disgusting, bloody mess of a night.

Ear Worms

However, one specific conversation I can morbidly recall verbatim.

Our usual nights out drinking on the town always had the same timeline, with the same conclusion. The same few pubs, with the same few people, having the same violent outbursts, eating the same curry and chips from the same kebab house, with the same fat, greasy-armed Greek dictator barking behind the counter for us to leave. (I don't know how they do things where you come from mate but it's called "having a laugh"). This was before the war. Back when everything was simple, fun, and exciting.

We start in The Forgotten Soldier. The strong stench of old beer and stale bleach hangs in the air. It is enough to make anybody's eyes weep. The warped carpet on the floor appears to be moving and I can't tell if I'm already pissed or there is some sort of infestation. An anonymous patron opts for Shakin' Stevens on the relatively unused jukebox, and I inwardly swear at the hidden

Ear Worms

inebriate for picking a tune. I'm well aware will haunt me until I've drowned it out in a large supply of budget lager, leaving me to wake up the next morning still swaying to its rhythm. To be honest with you, this squalid hole is about as bad a boozer as it can get, but we spend our little earnings here because it's cheap and cheerless. And not to mention the barmaid. She keeps us at arm's length, but that's fine by me. In my mind's eye, I can already see what she looks like under that rugby shirt. In fact, she ignores us so much, it's piss easy for us to lean over and pour our own pints. I know she knows we do this, but she couldn't care less (Good girl. That's how I view my job too). There are some schoolboy remarks scratched on to our table about a neighbouring football team, and although I couldn't give a flying fuck for the sport, I feel safe in this pub as a member of the home tribe.

Shakin' Stevens is still repeating, in his haunting echoey timbre, "you drive me cray-ayze".

Ear Worms

"So I don't get it, how did they catch you?" Shane belches as he downs the dregs of his Castlemaine XXXX. In the same frothy breath, he nods at me and points his empty glass at the emptier bar, tempting me to make a dash to nick the next round. I don't go get them just yet, there's still time. I need to finish my point.

"They didn't," I respond.

"So why did you get sacked from being my postie?"

It's bothering me he can't seem to comprehend my anecdote. It's not that complicated. Sometimes Shane really is dense. He's undeniably sweet, but honestly mate, it's time to step up your game. One of these days, you're going to get eaten alive.

I remember the first time I met him on the first day of secondary school. I spotted him walk through the door, wearing those stupid NHS milk bottles for glasses. He perfectly embodied the essence of the word "nerd." For reasons only

Ear Worms

known to Shane, he chose to sit right next to me. At first, I tried to ignore him but he shared some of his lemon bonbons with me which lightened the mood. Then we talked about football, and scary films, and I realised he wasn't too bad. However, I did make it very clear he wasn't to wear those specs around me.

    His mum always hated me but I could tell he hated her too. She was the perfect maternal figure that any kid could have asked for. Kind, attentive, smothering. It made me sick. She told Shane he wasn't to see me anymore but we still went to the park, and played knock-door-run, and nicked from the corner shop, and threw eggs at the brasses on the corner of Sutton Road. After he turned 16, the promise of manhood was creeping into our psyche, and controlling Shane proved too much of an arduous task for her, so at this point he was all mine.

Ear Worms

"Some old curtain twitcher reckons she saw me out of her window, but that's impossible," I continue.

"So you didn't nick the letters?"

"Irrelevant! It was impossible for her to see me!"

"I still don't get it mate. Did you take the letters or not?" Shane was beginning to tire with this line of questioning, and frankly so was I. He knows I did it, I know I did it. My boss knows I did it. The old cunt in the window knows I did. Pointless.

"Look, the letters were already in my pocket long before I got to her house. She just got lucky."

I feel myself getting hot under the collar so I let him know this conversation is over by abruptly heading to the bar without saying a word.

The barmaid had reappeared and was already pouring our beers. I try some small talk on her, but in return, all I receive is the wall. I know

Ear Worms

she doesn't like us because of our behaviour in here on our last venture but at least try and be polite! I begin to wonder to myself if she is even English and suddenly I find her repulsive. I make sure she sees me snarl as I return to my thirsty companion.

"Listen," I say as I take my first sip. This beer tastes different than before. It is extra warm and has a tangy aftertaste. I ponder what she might have done to our pints before I arrived at the bar. I still drink it though. Beer's beer.

"I've got an idea, and I want you to go in on it with me." I don't dance around it and choose to go straight for the jugular. "I'm thinking of joining the army."

Shane chokes on his jar of mystery brown liquid (it is unquestionably darker than the previous round). Wide-eyed, I can tell he is wondering if I'm joking.

"Sorry!?" Shane splutters.

Ear Worms

He knows I hate repeating myself so I refrain from using the same words.

"Don't be sorry mate, just come."

"No, I mean, what the fuck are you talking about!?"

"Why not? Lee went and apparently he is making some decent money."

"Who told you that?"

"Well, his mum told my mum."

"Lee's Mum also reckons he was head boy and doesn't know about any of his charges! She reckons he was volunteering in Africa with Bob Geldof. He was doing 3 months in Portland!"

To be honest, that is proper funny he told her that and it briefly makes me smile before I turn back to the matter at hand.

I cock my head slightly as I notice that infernal song is STILL repeating itself on the jukebox. How long does this tune go on for? Is it supposed to be ironic? No Stevens, YOU drive US crazy!

Ear Worms

"I'm gonna do it, I got nothing here. I can't wait to get out of this shit heap."

The booze is guiding my words now, but that doesn't make me wrong, it just makes me more confident.

"Come on, what's the real reason?"

"For Queen and country mate! For old Maggie! To send those Argie bastards back to where they came from!"

I see Shane's face twist at this comment and I realise I must've said something inexact. Shit, does that make sense? Aren't we going there? Subtly I move past t quicker than he can respond.

"Why don't we actually do something meaningful in our lives? For once!?"

I realise I'm shouting and I don't care. A pair of locals seated towards the rear of the pub briefly glance in the direction of the disturbance, only to promptly recognise their disinterest and resume nursing their sad pints of Guiness. I turn the volume up one more notch so Shane can hear

Ear Worms

me correctly over Shakin' Stevens' whining. I want Shane, (and the rest of the pub) to know how passionate I am, and judging by the flags on the ceiling I'm in the right place for it. A few more beers and my ambition will know no bounds. I am on the verge of becoming the most unstoppable force in here.

Shane remains calm. He is pensive and that really irks me. I'm itching for him to tell me he wants to go, but he likes this brief moment of power over me. He's always been this way, I guess the Yin to my Yang. That's our dynamic and that's the way we have always worked best. This is the real reason he has to come with me to the Falklands. He is the light, and I am the dark. He contemplates, and I act! He absolutely has to follow me to war. We are the perfect double act. The Two Ronnies, except only one of us has four eyes.

He throws the rest of his pint down his gullet, and I can see through the murky bottom of

Ear Worms

his glass that there is something floating in the dregs of it. I KNOW that cunt behind the bar tampered with our drinks. I still finish mine though.

There is a weird silence, not awkward or uncomfortable, but he's still taking time to think. I've had enough of this. I know what's coming next and I'm pretty sure I've already worked my magic. I've always been pretty convincing. Shane calls it 'unbearable persistence', his mum calls it 'peer pressure', but even more than ever, I don't care. Shakin' Stevens is starting up again and I have to get out of here. I decide to smash the final nail in the coffin as I finish the end of my questionable beer.

"Fuck it! You're doing it mate. Now come on, I want some chips."

Ear Worms
Chapter 3
War

Now, I sit here in my mouldy green armchair, watching whatever's showing on the box, ensuring that my alcohol levels remain sufficiently topped up to consistently see double. The stale cigarette smoke hangs in the air like a floating oil stain which is more entertaining than Blind Date on the tele.

    As I watch Cilla trying to match some thick tart from Wales with an even denser lad from Birmingham, I wonder why anyone bothers with any of this. Is this what people enjoy of an evening? Is this what I fought for? This is supposed to be prime-time tele. The best of the best in our schedule. Apparently, everyone watches this, but it means nothing. Nothing is happening on the show, and nothing will come from this. Sorry Cilla, ultimately, this holds no earthly significance.

Ear Worms

Nothing helps. I feel like modern technology hasn't yet been able to successfully find any sort of working remedy for this feeling. Guilt is an ancient force that has always been here and always will. Ultimately, guilt will suck me dry, and ultimately, it will win.

I'm bored. Eternally bored!

The sensation in my gut returns, an ever-present reminder that I've killed my only friend. It has become my sole companion, pulsing in slow, deliberate rhythms, often reaching its zenith in the silence of the night. Each day bleeds into the next, but when the guilt reaches its climax, it seems impossible to maintain the facade of a functioning, well-rounded member of society. The pain always starts in the pit of my stomach, gradually rising and rising, and when it reaches its summit, I can feel it from the tips of all my extremities, and in my eyelids and lips.

They used to call it 'shell-shocked,' but now they have some fancy acronym that doesn't

Ear Worms

make me feel any better. I prefer the term "Shell-Shocked." The words get to the heart of the sensation. It's brutal and leaves a bitter taste in your mouth. Still, it doesn't matter on the language; no wording can change what I feel or what I did. Nothing can alter that.

I stopped the drugs they gave me almost as quickly as they were issued. They weren't helping. In fact, they were making it worse. After I stopped seeing Shane, the shame continued to grow. I wanted to be confronted with what had happened. They wanted me to forget, but I didn't want that. This was my punishment that I had accepted long ago.

The group sessions proved to be an excruciating experience for all participants. We were coerced into discussing our emotions and our thoughts, blah blah blah. It all seemed rather monotonous. Most faces made only a single appearance before vanishing from the sessions altogether. Before long, I joined the ranks of those absent without leave. The entire affair was deeply humiliating and thoroughly uncomfortable. Given the choice, I'd prefer to self-medicate with whatever the most affordable bottle behind the counter had to offer.

Cilla screams, "Surprise, surprise!" for no apparent reason, and I jolt back into reality. For a split second, it felt as if the pain had peaked and was beginning to wane, but no, she is still there, forever rising like a blocked sewer in a storm. Eventually, something will break. After the isolated village has flooded and the rain shows no sign of relenting; after the sandbags laid in front of the local post office have been submerged and are no longer protecting anything from the ever-rising shit and piss water; after people's livelihoods have been stripped away from them and the insurance won't pay.

But there is nothing else that can break. I'm left with my perpetual, ever-expanding pain.

Ear Worms

It wasn't the blood, or bones, or bits of entrails or brain matter that bothered me. It wasn't retreating as fast as I could through a minefield, with Lance Corporal whatever-his-name-was raining down on me in smaller and smaller parts. It wasn't lying in the mud, hearing the screams of the young foreign forces slitting the throats of my sleeping regiment, wondering if my number was due at any moment. I don't even need to tell you what the reason is, but his name is always at the front of my thoughts.

I wince at the thought of Shane, and my mind races to that night. It wasn't solely the rain, the wind, or the cold; it was the ruthless combination of all three elements that made our time there utterly wretched. It felt as though sharp razors were relentlessly cutting into our eyes as we lay face down in the dirt, anxiously awaiting the command.

They called it the Battle for Mount Langdon, but the word "battle" is doing a lot of

Ear Worms

unnecessary work in that title. Massacre is probably a bit too strong, but the truth is, it wasn't far off a walk in the park.

We had an ideal tactical position above them in the mountains, and our foes were none the wiser. We watched them through the scopes on our rifles, play cards and laugh, utterly oblivious to their impending doom. We felt confident. We were going to obliterate these pigs, and there wasn't a fucking thing they could do about it. Shooting fish in a barrel.

Shane was quivering next to me. It's difficult to determine whether it was the circumstances or the environment, but regardless, I instinctively wrapped my arm around him in an attempt to put him at ease. We locked eyes. He didn't have to tell me, but I could read him like a book. He's petrified.

"Stay behind me mate. I'm a better marksman than you. I'll keep you safe," I try to reassure him.

Ear Worms

I don't think he heard the words. They forced Shane to wear those thick-lensed glasses, now speckled with raindrops. Even if he were an expert sharpshooter, there was no chance he'd be able to hit his target under these conditions.

Shane's still shaking, and my knees go warm. I realise he has pissed himself.

This was the point I should have convinced him to return to base. This was when we should have retreated, together. Taken whatever punishment that the powers that be deemed appropriate. What were we doing here? We're not killers.

Hindsight really is a fucker.

Except, with all this in mind, no amount of whimpering or telepathic complaining was going to have me miss my moment of glory.

I decided not to tell him now how outraged I was at the piss; I would bank that until we were back and dry at base. Maybe I would have forgotten by then but I doubt it.

Ear Worms

There are several flashes, and I can hear the undeniable popping of gunfire in the immediate distance. The assault has started. We await our signal, but it can't be long. In an instant, the sound of thousands of bullets discharging takes over this beautiful hillside area. A constant "tap-tap-tap" echoes throughout the hills, and our adversaries are falling quicker than they can pick up their arms. A whizzing noise flies inches past my ear, and I do all I can to try to push myself lower into the ground. Through the precipitation, I am just able to spy where the shooting came from. The top of a tiny head behind an oil barrel is poking out, with the tip of his rifle pointing directly at us, Shane makes a noise resembling a whimper, but I have no time for his complaining. I give him a quick kick, and he finally shuts up. This is my fish in a barrel, and I have my crosshairs locked directly on the top of his cover position; all I need is for him to rear his ugly little head one more time. I exhale and assess all conditions. The wind is really billowing, and I

Ear Worms

know I'm going to need lady luck on my side if I'm going to make any sort of impact. Another flash, but this one goes way high. The first shot was a fluke! He doesn't know what he is doing. I have the upper hand, which gives me the confidence to complete my task. The gale briefly drops. I close one eye and squeeze the trigger.

Red mist spews from behind the barrel.

This is the final shot of the assault, followed by a brief silence and the unmistakable roar of British men triumphantly cheering. I remember this sound from the terraces with my dad as a boy. Grown men, never previously displaying any emotion, crying and hugging. Before I turn to Shane, the undeniable coppery smell of blood in the air enters my nostrils, and my stomach drops.

There lies Shane, body still warm. The area where his face should be is a swamp of pink flesh, blood, bone, and teeth. The hole through his face looks as if a grapefruit, traveling at the speed of sound, had impacted it. His jaw is nowhere to be seen, and his tongue is now inside out and licking the back of his neck. Over the sound of the wind and rain, I hear blood bubbling out of his open trachea. The crown of his head has seemingly separated from his skull, only connected on the left side, reminiscent of a jack-in-the-box lid opening on a hinge.

Shane is not only dead, he has been obliterated. What I see now will be the everlasting image I will have of him. I scream. What am I looking at? Is this real? Have I slipped into some horror novel or am I actually here? Where is the glory I've been desperately seeking? I stop screaming to take a breath. And I scream again. And again. And again.

Once there is no more breath in me to scream, I stand up, propping myself up with my rifle. I know my foe has departed this world, but that isn't enough for me. I need vengeance. I abandon my only friend's remains and walk to my target. It takes longer than I anticipate, and I realise

Ear Worms

how far away we were from each other. Either lucky, or impressive shooting. From both sides.

    I arrive at the barrel and look over to see the bastard lying in the mud, face up, eyes closed, using the inside of his skull as a pillow. Why didn't his face look like Shane's? All this foreign cunt received was a small bullet hole under his eye. That's it? I kick the body, and when I do this, I notice the strangest thing. His lips are still moving. Is he still alive? No, he can't be. A pale husk of his former self, brains emitted ten yards behind him.

    I clip off my bayonet from my rifle and crouch down next to his face. He is still muttering something, but it's in Spanish or whatever they speak here. I don't care. I go to wipe the dirt off his face with my knife, but I realise it's not mud. It's some sort of markings. Tattoos? His face is cold, but he is still talking. I stand up and kick him again. His legs are locked into place. To any other onlooker, you would assume he is deceased, but he is still talking, appearing very much alive.

Ear Worms

I crouch down to his level, knife in hand, and gently slip it behind his right ear. A realisation dawns on me that I hadn't sharpened the blade since it came into my possession, leaving me acutely aware of its dullness. Good!

I try to saw at the flesh, but not much happens at first. I pull at the ear with my left hand to make the skin taut, and this helps somewhat, but the task is proving more difficult than it appeared, especially without the proper tools for the job. The blade eventually slips halfway in, and I end up tearing the thing right off, taking half of his cheek with it, and what I see shocks me. Not the blood or gore, but the lack of it. What remains on the left-hand side of his face is his pale pink flesh, exposing some white of his skull and the first couple of top molars. As I look back, his lips are still moving. But now, his eyes are open. Were they always open? Is he looking at me?

What does the body do after death? Maybe it does move? Except Shane didn't. The man with

Ear Worms

the tattoos' lips are still moving though. Enough is enough. I stand up and empty my clip into his face. He now is a mirror of Shane. No lips left to move.

A feeling of cathartic peace starts to take over, and somehow I feel I have made amends. This piece of shit can suffer in the afterlife, and I am safe in the knowledge it was me that placed him there. My new prize discreetly nestles inside my damp sock, hidden from prying eyes. It gradually slithers down my ankle, settling at my heel, and a sudden epiphany strikes me: I must find a dry place for it, and soon. The last thing I want is for someone else's skin to become mouldy alongside my own.

Ear Worms
Chapter 4
The Tub

So here I sit, riddled with all sorts of feelings of shame. I feel like I've been sitting here all night, just thinking, reminiscing, dissecting my thoughts.

As the showy, Vegas-styled theme music of Blind Date's credits roll onscreen, I unsuccessfully reach down the side of my chair for my newest, loyal friend, the budget corner shop vodka. But it's not there. Bemused, I look over and notice the bottle has fallen over, and its migraine-inducing contents have spilled on the floor. I stare over to an image of a glass body, with its murky, alcoholic brains dashed over the already-soiled carpet. I clench my fist and attempt to grab it, with the intention of launching it across the room, but I can't seem to muster the energy.

There was another time when a Saturday would have involved myself and Shane running amok around town, causing a nuisance. Trying to determine the highlight of my existence, my peak of happiness, can be a tricky one. Yet, in retrospect, I can confidently declare, that was it.

This is my Saturday now…

And Sunday…

And Monday…

And every day ending in 'Y'.

A relentless loop of remorse, temporarily dulled by booze, fading into unconsciousness, and then reawakening to what happened, perpetuates endlessly. Sometimes I wonder if I had died on that battlefield, and if this is some sort of hell. I get no gratification from this thought, but I guess it's an interesting idea if true.

Of course, Shane is still with me; he's shown his face a few times tonight (or lack thereof). Sometimes in the corner of the room, sometimes next to two other mindless contestants in high chairs on the TV with Cilla. Sometimes I know he is in the room without actually seeing

Ear Worms

him. I can smell him from that night. The mud, coppery blood, piss, and gunpowder.

I stub out my last cigarette, put my hand in my front jean pocket, and pull out my "lucky charm". The ear. Everyone was looting bodies that night, taking what they could for themselves. I know a few of my squad saw me too, but largely most of the team were turning a blind eye. Well, almost everybody. Some little rat ran up to Sarge and told him what I had done. I know the boss was too elated about the recent landslide victory to actually care, but now he had been burdened with the truth he was forced to show his authority. So I was promptly and swiftly detained and thrown out of the forces. I was lucky to elude military prison. I don't think they wanted knowledge of my personal war crime released to the public, so a quick military beheading barrelled my way. We couldn't besmirch the victory of The Battle of Mount Langdon. It was easier to send me on my merry

Ear Worms

path to self-destruction and let that be that, and this decision suited me just fine.

I play around with the contents of my pocket. It's hard now, dried like a prune, and has a funny musky smell to it. I left the earring coarsely stabbed into it. A small blue stud. This artefact is my vengeance. It reminds me that it wasn't all for nothing. I took one of those bastards down, and now his soul belongs to me. My very own solo collection of the essence of mankind. It used to make me feel at peace every time I held it, but now I'm not so sure. I don't know what I feel. Nothing brings Shane back to this world. What's the point of any of this? I poke the mummified ear back down into my pocket and try to let my body relax enough to pass out. I'm certainly drunk enough, but that putrid smell is once again entering my nostrils. Mud, blood, piss, and gunpowder.

This is going to be another sleepless night.

"Right, that's it!" I say to nobody as I struggle to get to my feet. I fall into the ashtray,

Ear Worms

knocking a week's worth of fag butts to the ground.

I eventually find the bathroom and ping the cord to the light. The room was once completely white, now a deep shade of yellowy cream. The bulb flickers and struggles to keep its enthusiasm as it brings illumination into this dank squalid room. Eventually, the light settles but it's dim. I stare at my bloodshot tired eyes in the mirror. My face's ambition to grow an unkempt beard is attempting to show itself, but my hormones haven't yet allowed me to even look like a man. I look like shit. Everyone I've bumped into has said it. Mum has complained down the phone to me that I haven't visited her in a while, but I don't want her to see me like this. She can remember the person I used to be, before the war.

I slump onto the toilet seat, reaching out to turn on the taps, allowing the bathtub to gradually fill with water. With my head in my hands, I'm trying to think. I need a pen. Where in my house is a pen? Every house has a pen. The thought of

Ear Worms

actually searching is enough to make me pull the plug on the whole idea (not to mention the bathtub), but I know deep down I need to stay focused. This drive leads me to open the toothpaste cap and squirt some onto my finger, and it dawns on me that this is a new tube. When did I buy this?

    I smear the red, white, and blue paste onto the mirror and spell out the two words in big letters across the entire frame. The mint smell offends my nostrils but has partially replaced the smell of mud, blood, piss, and gunpowder.

    I'm almost done now, just one last step. The water is overflowing across the bath and spilling onto the mould-lined tiles. The top of the bathwater has a layer of dust and spiders, and is now making its descent down the waterfall, and soon throughout my house. Seeing double makes everything so much harder, but I'm almost there. Just need something electrical now.

Ear Worms

After a quick trip to the shed to grab the radio and the extension cord, I'm all set. This is going to hurt. A lot.

Oh well! Fuck it.

As I switch the radio on, that wretched song from the pub is playing and I wince. Shakin' Stevens! Great! This is the last song I ever listen too! Thanks again God. A brief flashback to a moment when I had the power to change the course of events darts into my mind, and I shake it out.

I don't know why but I check the time (as if that's going to make any difference). It's 12:02 AM (when did it get so late?)

Fully clothed, I step into the tub and lie down, making sure to hold Shakin' Stevens' whiny voice above my head. The water is freezing, and I almost step out. I chuckle to myself that I have to be comfortable to commit suicide. Shane is here (of course), standing above me. His silhouette is framed by the light leaking through the gaping hole in his head. It is impossible to tell what his face is

Ear Worms

portraying, as he hasn't got one, but I sense he is urging me to finally get this done.

Over the tinny racket of Mr. Stevens, I can hear Shane's disembodied voice say, "fuck it, you're doing it."

I let the radio tumble into the depths of my murky bathtub.

Ear Worms
Chapter 5
Try Harder

Wow! That sucked! Of course, it didn't work. A quick death would be too good for me. I don't deserve that. I'm unsure of what exactly happened, but here I sit, like a boiled slice of bacon. I can feel my hair standing up on end, and I imagine I look like a picture from Looney Tunes (I wonder if Shane saw my skeleton?). Even in the dark, I try to somehow see around the room, to sense if he is still here, but the familiar feeling of isolation has returned. The only thing I can smell is me.

    The pain was monumental. It's hard to explain, but I guess it felt how static looks on a weak aerial signal. Every fibre of me could feel the surge of every single volt. I felt electric spasming from my toenails all the way to my teeth.

    The actual act of dropping the radio, the split second decision, was as clear as day in my

Ear Worms

head. This was the right thing to do. Now it's over, and I'm still here on this earth, in the dark, in a cold bathtub, reeking of singed hair and burnt fat. Why did I choose this method of suicide? I really, REALLY don't want to do anything like that again. The 'end' makes sense, but I need to streamline the 'means'.

    I try to check the time on my wristwatch, in some misguided hope that it's still 12:02 and maybe I succeeded. If I actually died, then time would stand still, right? Maybe it did work and this is what death is? Maybe the reaper slipped in and out without myself or Shane ever noticing? Everything is blurry, so I wipe my eyes, and the residual liquid left on my fingers is warm, with an undeniable metallic smell. Why are my eyes bleeding? I splash the putrid water on my face to try and rid my sight of its obstruction, but everything is still blurry. I strain my eyes, and I can just about make out the harsh, neon red digital numbers on my Casio watch.

Ear Worms

It is 12:09.

"Fuck," I meekly mutter to myself.

The whole ordeal went on for 7 minutes. 7 minutes of searing pain, passing out, and being jolted awake in perpetuity. Surely my kill should have been instantaneous? What did I do wrong? Why didn't it work?

As I attempt to drag myself out of the tub, my fatigue consumes me, and I let my body slip back into the water like a dead rat. I lie there for a long time with my face just breaking the water. Something drifting on the surface bumps into my cheek. I can't see it, but I can smell it. I must have released my bowels at some point. I've had worse. I don't care enough to recoil or even push it away.

I'm glad it's dark. I don't want to be confronted by the state I'm in. The smell of the water is enough to make me gag, but I am unable to produce any stomach contents. I guess my innards are all in here somewhere. I recall a time when I tried to boil a shoulder of pork. I didn't

Ear Worms

know how to cook, but me and Shane thought it would be nice to eat something that wasn't a take-away or spam sandwiches, but our ambition clearly outweighed our ability. We swiftly forgot about the bubbling meat and ended up in the pub. Six hours later I returned to my bed and passed out, stinking of all sorts of booze. Another 10 hours after that I am greeted in the kitchen with a pot of putrid, half-reduced creamy brown water, with a top layer of scum and a rancid, withered pig part in the middle.

That's me. Burnt, over-cooked pork, stinking to high heaven.

I'm still alive though. I think about letting myself slip under, but I'm not convinced that my body's natural response to the sewer water will let me stay under for the required time for the deed to be done. Eventually, I am able to summon the energy to fall out of the tub, and I lie on the bathroom floor. My body gives up once more, and I see black.

Ear Worms

Light again, and this time it's morning. The birds are singing their incessant chirpy songs. Of course they are jovial and carefree; they're barely even conscious of their surroundings. Just living off impulse and instinct. No boredom, no love or hate, no wars, no PTSD, no actual life. I'd be singing too if all I did was fly, eat, and fuck.

The tiles are freezing, but I can't seem to feel them underneath me. I know it's wet and cold on my skin, but my senses refuse to actually acknowledge this, my brain merely recognising the conditions. It's an odd but not unpleasant sensation. Maybe I've burnt off all my nerves? That'll make my next attempt easier.

My eyes have regained their sight, and I'm very aware not to glance in the mirror. If I looked like shit before I went in the tub, there is no way I'm allowing myself to see the freak show I've turned myself into. I can see all the matter I've left floating in the tub from last night's antics, and I both laugh and gag at the same time. A mixture of

Ear Worms

bile and blood shoots from my mouth onto my chest. In my peripherals, I see my miniature suicide note I smeared on the mirror last night.

'For Shane'

I don't allow my eyes to focus on the two undead freaks behind it.

I've got to take these clothes off, and when I find the opportunity, they are going in the incinerator. Fire burns everything clean.

FIRE BURNS EVERYTHING! A rare lightbulb moment pops into my head, and this thought warms my heart. That's how I'll do it next!

A frightful notion lingers in the back of my mind. The radio in the tub was more than excruciating; this time round, fire would be a lot worse. Setting myself ablaze would definitely do the trick, but the only lesson I've taken from this failed suicide is to make sure next time, it's instant.

Before I strip, I reach into my front jean pocket and take out my most prized possession. There are small black scorch marks striking out

Ear Worms

from the earring and tattooing itself all the way to the ridge of the ear like black lightning. I wonder if he felt that in the afterlife too?

I drag myself from the bathroom to my squalid little living room, naked and wet with all sorts of biological spewings. I spot the screwed-up fag packet on the floor and curse God once more. A smoke right now would at least alleviate some pain.

The TV is still on from last night, and Peter Sissons is discussing something to do with the miners' strikes. His dulcet tone is somehow soothing, and, although I'm not listening to his words, the noise he is making relaxes me.

Shane is behind the TV set, shaking his head. I can just about see the end of his tongue behind his skull, by each ear as he gestures his cranium from side to side, showing his displeasure at my still-beating pulse.

I start to think about what I have done. Do I still want to go through with it? Last night was

Ear Worms

really awful. Pain nobody is ever supposed to endure. A radio in the bathtub would have killed anyone else. It must have been a bleak twist of fate. An unfortunate and curious combination of conditions within my body that resulted in my survival. One in a million chance. Lightning never strikes twice, right? I won't have to go through the pain again. The next time my attempt will work. I think back to the feeling of tranquility I had in the moment before I dropped the radio. Do I still want to go through with this?

    It is odd that I'm still here, though. I rack my brains to make any sort of sense of this, but no rhyme or reason is manifesting. I try to lock eyes with the faceless figure behind the TV screen, but it's tricky to know where his eyes are.

    "Why, Shane? Why am I still here?"

    Shane stares back without a word or a gesture.

Ear Worms

Maybe I'm lucky? Maybe I'm destined for something greater! No. That's absurd. I'm just incredibly unlucky.

The idea of fire jumps back to mind. I've got lighter fluid under the sink. I think it'll be enough to douse myself, but if I'm honest, the act of self-immolation frightens me. I'm in such a weakened state right now; I don't think my heart would be able to take the impact. But isn't that the point?

I sit and think, and I have another lightbulb moment.

Hanging! We've been killing ourselves for millions of years in that way. That's a classic for a reason.

Ear Worms

Chapter 6
The Tree

A few days pass, maybe a week. I don't really move from my chair. I struggle to find any energy from my ordeal the other night. I haven't eaten, but I'm not hungry.

I know I don't have any rope in my house, and I'm struggling to think of anything I can use that can take my weight. I've worked out the place for it though. The old dying oak tree in the garden is sturdy enough. The only issue I can foresee is if a neighbour catches the act from their window. Community spirit (or the lack thereof) will work in my favour. Nobody really cares about anybody else around here, so, as long as I commit the deed at night, everything should go to plan. All I need is a rope.

Once I trudge outside to the garden, I wrap my belt around the branch of the tree and grasp it

Ear Worms

with both hands, lifting my feet off the ground. I'm there for a good 30 seconds before… Snap! I hit the ground hard and my head bounces off a protruding root. It hurts. A lot. My vision becomes blurry. I wonder if I'm lucky enough to die from this stupid fall, without even trying, but there goes that word again. 'Luck'. They could write a sitcom about my misfortunes.

    I stand up, shake it off, and stumble back into my depressing dwellings.

    I didn't want another embarrassing misfire like last time, even if it was just for an audience of Shane. Eventually, I am able to mobilise the energy to walk to the hardware store and purchase the rope designed for towing cars. The man behind the counter asks me what car I am intending on using it for, to see if the cord is compatible, before cutting his sentence short. I look up to realise he is aghast at the state of me. I haven't looked in the mirror since the night in the tub, but I know I must be something grotesque. I peer down onto the counter

Ear Worms

and a large clump of my hair is drifting down towards my purchase. I shrug don't respond. Quickly, I pay and leave before I have to say any words or even collect my change (I won't need it).

Back home, I try the rope on another branch and it holds. This will work just fine.

I try to anticipate every potential outcome that will result in my survival, but nothing else springs to mind. The only anomaly I can predict is a nosy neighbour, but I've been out here watching for a couple of days now. Nobody even looks out of the windows. The risk of being spotted is minimal to none. Everyone's personal privacy is deemed too sacred around here.

Tonight's the night.

I feel like a kid at Christmas. I'm so excited. Giddy and full of vigour. I bounce to the shop and buy myself one final pack of fags and some more white spirit with a label claiming "vodka". I nod to all shocked passerby on my walk home and they must think I've won the lottery, or

Ear Worms

finally shared a kiss with a long sought-after love interest. Nope, sorry guys, I don't entertain such fortune, tonight I'll make my own luck.

It's starting to get dark, and I'm staring out of my window at the brutal oak, naked of leaves. It's mighty and ancient. The original intended branch is still laid on the ground near its roots, so instead I'll have to use the one higher. Its still high enough to hang my neck from.

I wonder how many other individuals have been strung up and strangled on this? I can't be the only one? That thing has been there for centuries. Maybe a scorned lover from the Victorian era met their untimely end on it. Or perhaps it's older than that? A strapping young Saxon lynched a poor old fat monk on this tree, requiring several Vikings to drag his portly figure high enough for his neck to snap.

That's a good point, actually. I wonder if my neck will snap? That's the intention, but I'm well-versed in my own fortune to know that I'm

Ear Worms

not that lucky, however what a nice treat that would be. Something sweet after all these sickly few years I've had to endure.

In the kitchen, I'm playing with the rope in my hands. I don't know how to make a noose. How do people just have this knowledge in films and TV programmes? I decide on just the basic knot that kids use when learning to tie their shoelaces. Double knot though (I'm not an idiot). This has to work. I tug it. It's sturdy. There's no movement in the bindings. Confidence is brimming from every atom of my being.

I make the decision to head out around 2 in the morning. Why would anybody be in their gardens then? The grass is dewy and I enjoy the smell, my last final pleasure in this life. The ground under the tree isn't flat enough to support my stool for very long without slipping, but I guess that's the whole point.

Shane is here with me, willing me on. I can sense he is around here somewhere. I feel he is

Ear Worms

excited to finally spend real time with me, without the separation of my soul.

The branch I'm using is several feet higher than I can reach. It's a lot harder to swing the rope over in the dark, and the bottle of moonshine coursing through my veins isn't making it any easier. But of course, I eventually manage.

The loop dangles in front of my face and I can barely see it. I attach myself to the mechanism and lock myself in. A final thought runs through my mind. Why didn't I leave a note? Why would I write a note? The bathroom mirror still has my final thoughts on it, and I don't feel any different. Who's going to actually care anyways. Maybe my mum. I feel bad for her, but I feel worse about Shane. This seems to be my only way to make amends. I think she will understand. Maybe she will blame ol' Maggie and the war effort. Maybe she will blame dad and my violent upbringing. Hopefully, she will just blame me. She should do.

I thumb the ear in my pocket.

Ear Worms

Right, enough of this, let's go.

I kick the stool and I tumble (no snap, I told you), with my neck catching my weight. My feet less than ten centimetres from the floor.

I didn't account for the rope flexing down, but it should still do the job. If I point my feet to the ground I might even be able to support myself so I keep my knees bent, with my toes pointing to the sky.

The knot around my neck is tight. No chance of slipping out (who needs a noose?). I can feel my windpipe crushing. I won't ever breathe another breath again. The feeling is causing great discomfort, but I try to meditate past it. Darkness starts to creep in around my vision and I welcome it.

Shane stares blankly at me through nonexistent eyes. That is the last thing I see before everything goes black. Then the sound of the cars in the street and the wind rustling quiets until they are no more than a muffle.

Ear Worms

I smell the mud, piss, blood and gunpowder and this time I welcome the stench. I'm looking forward to my reunion with Shane.

There I hang, in pitch black and complete silence. My mind tricks me into thinking I can hear Shakin' Stevens again and I feel myself start to cry. I choke it down and let The Reaper visit once more.

Ear Worms
Chapter 7
The Garden

Just as quickly as I am carried off to my eternal night, I drift back into the harsh light of the morning. The smell of the dew hits again, and I slowly open my eyes. The hopeless realisation of my repeated circumstance starts to set in. I'm still hanging from the tree in my dank unkempt garden.

My bleary eyes begin to widen, and I can make out the cruel sight of the morning, informing the rest of civilisation to start their day again.

Morning!? I must be dead this time. How long have I been here?

I try to focus my eyes, and I can just make out the rough outline of my residence. Everything looks the same as last night? Maybe the underworld is just a cruel trick by Lucifer. Maybe when we die we don't know that we are dead? Is anybody even here?

Ear Worms

The swaying begins to make me feel nauseous. I have to get down. I stretch my feet as much as I can, just enough for the tip of my shoes to touch the ground, which relieves just enough pressure off the rope to help me untie the knot, toes tickling the same protruding root I smashed my head against a few nights prior. I hope nobody is watching this. What a pathetic sight this must be.

The house on my left has its curtains open in the kitchen window. Were they open or closed last night? I think they were closed? Surely if somebody had seen me, they would have dialled 999? Of course, this is assuming anybody actually cared. It would be a lot easier to turn a blind eye and let someone else deal with the depressed hanging neighbour next door.

My fingers are just able to grasp at the knot, but there is still too much pressure. I can't do this on my own. I need help. I wish somebody did see me. I wish just this once somebody cared.

Ear Worms

It's a frosty morning, and the sweet smell of dew from the previous night has laid a white veil over all the brown greenery. To my surprise, I notice I can't see my breath in front of me. Hang on, I can't breathe! So I am dead, ergo… this is my hell?!

Cars are passing on the road outside. I can hear a small altercation on the street, resulting in some indecipherable blasphemes and some honking. Some light joshing by local schoolboys about someone's mother is just audible.

I didn't expect cars in hell.

I didn't expect mild road rage in hell.

I didn't expect childish banter in hell.

I didn't expect the delightful smell of dew in hell.

Where's all the fire and brimstone?

This is still the same stinking, ugly world I was born in, and I am still yet to receive my rebirth.

Ear Worms

Still tugging at the knot, I curse myself for making it so damn tight. I can smell Shane behind me. It's all well and good having your friend haunt you from beyond the grave, but at least give me a fucking hand here mate. This is exhausting. I let myself hang again and try to give death another go.

I dangle.

I sway.

I try to close my eyes and succumb to the darkness but it's too bright out here.

Nobody is at any of the windows. I hear parents telling off their unruly kids a few doors to the right, and I hear car doors slam and reluctant engines burst into life as they take their occupants to their ultimately meaningless jobs. The sun inches slightly across the sky, and the air begins to feel more like the afternoon.

Why am I not dead? This makes no sense. I assumed the ordeal in the bathtub was some fluke. Maybe you can't actually die from frying yourself in your bath. Maybe that's just a ploy created by

Ear Worms

films and books for an exciting drama. But this?! This should have worked.

Boredom coupled with the spectre of a hangover starts to edge their way over me. My temples start to pulse, but I'm not convinced whether it's my suffocation or the thinly veiled paint stripper I guzzled last night.

There is a territorial spat between a dog and an ambitious cat somewhere in the vicinity. The deep roaring of the hound echoes right through my ears, and I can feel it in my bones.

None of this makes sense. The dog, the cat, the fight, it's all real. This is the same reality I tried to vacate last night. Yet here I swing, somewhere between life and death, unable to commit to either state. 'Purgatory' feels too fantastical an expression to claim I can be living through, but I'm struggling to find any other wording for my current predicament.

The afternoon comes and goes, and I spend my entire time thinking about why I'm still here.

Ear Worms

Occasionally I try to shout out for help, but my vocal cords seem to have been damaged in my unsuccessful suicide. Nobody would come anyways.

As the evening starts to make its way to me, I wonder if I still have the ear in my pocket. I attempt to look down, but the rope is holding my head in such a way that it is making the viewpoint impossible. I meditate on why I feel so attached to that ear. Does it remind me of Shane? No, it reminds me of my vengeance. The man with the tattooed face deserved everything he got. He was lucky that's all I took. Just like me, I recall that he was alive before he was dead too. Even with his brains all Jackson Pollock-ed behind him, murmuring to himself something in Spanish. Should have cut the tattoos off his face too, kept that instead.

Quick as a flash, it all comes to mind. All the images smash into my head at once. Why can't I kill myself?

Ear Worms

Was this his doing? The man with the tattooed face? I can't be cursed! Curses aren't real, are they? What was he saying as he was lying in the mud, brains in a halo around his scalp? Why would he curse me with immortality? That's a gift, isn't it? The Fountain of Youth and all that.

Panic is beginning to set in. The one thing I always thought I had control over, and now I can't even kill myself. This is absurd.

No, I'll tell you what is absurd, swinging from a tree by your neck, staring at a ghost of your mutilated best friend.

How can someone live forever? That's completely unfathomable. Where is the line drawn? Even if I was immortal, that can't actually mean 'forever', can it? The reason for my unintended success in life is that both my attempts have been too half-hearted. I appear to be taking the word 'commit' out of 'commit suicide'. If the body is destroyed, then how can I live past that? If I ever

Ear Worms

get out of this, I just need to make sure that my last attempt is absolute. Destroy the body.

SNAP!

A delayed neck snap? No. Some sort of divine intervention decides to come to my aid, and suddenly I am lying on the floor, scrambling to liberate my neck from this infernal knot. I don't know why the branch finally decided to snap, but I'm thankful it did.

I decide to leave the device wrapped around my neck and trudge into the kitchen, with the rope and branch in tow. I'm off to grab a knife and cut the fucking thing off.

That's it! A knife!!!!

Ear Worms
Chapter 8
The Blade

Right, I've had enough of this. This is beyond silly now. This one is going to be quick. No thought. Just do it.

Eternal life? Get to fuck. That's not real. I'm not having that.

As I stand over the kitchen sink, rope and tree still in tow, I stare at myself in my reflection from the window. Shane's next to me, and it's hard to tell which one of us is the ghost. We both look like zombies. I gaze through his smashed cherry pie of a face, and I know it this time. This attempt is going to work. This really is going to happen now! I KNOW it. I can feel it in my gut. No fucking around.

I recall this feeling just once before. Shane and I were passing a casino on our way home from

Ear Worms

another drunken escapade, and the number 17 bus zooms past us, Shane grabs my arm.

"Right, come on mate, that's it. I've seen that number loads today. 17 is coming in." Before I know it, we are stumbling our way inside the casino and making a beeline for the roulette table.

Shane is trying to explain where else he has seen the number that day, but I'm not listening. I don't need to, I already know he is right. I can feel it too. 17 is coming up next on the dealer's table. It's not a premonition, but more of a pure and simple fact. I know this as clear as day. No messing about now, just act.

The table is full of chancers, making a small amount of chips, but ultimately losing it all to the house. Due to Shane's smaller frame, he is able to squeeze his way to the front, where he tosses a crumpled 5 pound note on number 17, just as the croupier calls "no more bets."

The ball does its tiny jig over every number, eventually settling itself home on number

Ear Worms

17. He won! Instinct prevailed! Shane snatches his winnings and quickly runs over to cash out.

Nobody else won on that table this round. Just us. I remember thinking how cool we must have looked, like James Bond or something (well, at least we thought we did). Three or four other punters rush over to us to ask what we think is coming in next, but we just laugh and walk out £185 richer.

As sure as I knew that number 17 was next on the dealer's table, I'm sure that this next attempt is going to claim my life. Hex or not, I won't be able to survive what's coming.

Is slitting my wrists my best idea? The thought of fire still swims about in my mind, but right now, I'm here, with the right tool for the job, and there is no more time for any more thoughts. No time to change my mind, or convince myself otherwise, just have to take the leap.

I know how to do this. No technical knots to try and navigate. No pansy left-to-right action.

Ear Worms

Cut deep and true down the soft part of the inside of my arm.

As the blade draws south from my elbow to my wrist, I notice how the cold steel feels against my bones. It sends a chill all the way up my spine, but I continue. Now the right arm. I swap the knife into my left hand and realise I can no longer grasp the handle of the blade very well. Not only has the blood spurting out of my new gaping wound made the knife slippery, but I've lost all sense in my extremities. I make my second attempt, but this incision is not as deep.

Now, the final step. Fumbling the knife like a live fish, I eventually manage to grip the blade with both hands and draw it across my Adam's apple, using my bruise from the rope as a trace. Before I'm all the way across, I drop the knife. It doesn't matter. Even this half job will do the trick.

Warm, crimson blood is now spurting in all directions, and the trauma my body is going through is enough to block the searing agony bubbling up from my arms and throat. I must be in shock. In my reflection, I can see the visceral raw damage I have dragged my body through, and now the real test can begin.

I start to feel faint and wait for the warm embrace of my final exit.

Collapsing to the floor, I smile at Shane looking over me. I barely have enough energy in me to take out my trophy and hold it, but I manage. Hopefully, I can smuggle it across the river Styx.

But I don't pass out. Nothing happens. I lie, curled in the foetal position until I get cold. The deep red pool around me starts to solidify, and I give up on giving up. It appears the man with the tattooed face has domain over my life and death.

I am cursed. That's a hat trick now. There is no other explanation, no matter how fantastical the spell sounds.

I don't know how long I lie there, but I see the pale blue hue of the morning light again, as it softly edges into my kitchen. I haven't been hungry

Ear Worms

for days, and I haven't needed to evacuate my bladder or bowels since I made my homemade bathtub, human soup. I'm not even convinced I've slept since then either, it's been more like closing my eyes and waiting. All my usual bodily habits have ceased, yet I'm still here. On this sticky, red lake of a kitchen floor.

    I try to contemplate the alternative. Attempting to actually live my life. That can't be so bad, can it? Maybe I'll be happy? Perhaps this is a blessing, and should I succeed in completely reversing my situation, the man with the tattooed face may find himself spinning in his grave. However, despite all this pain and trauma I've endured through my various unsuccessful attempts on my life, nothing is as agonising as the remorse I still feel for Shane every moment I am still breathing. That thought scares me more than any of my suicide attempts. I HAVE to destroy my body. But how can you kill what cannot be killed?

Ear Worms

Eventually I move. The morning has taken hold now, and I hear my neighbours boiling their kettles for their ritualistic morning brew. Someone turns their morning radio on, and if it isn't that fucking Shakin' Stevens' song again! It's unbearable! I have to get out of here! I stand up and change my clothes, put on my coat, and head for Rufus Blake Halls. The stature of that building eclipses all others in this town, more than enough to complete my final suicide attempt. Just as I shut my door, I realise I've left my keys on the other side of the locked threshold. It doesn't matter, I won't need those where I'm going. The only thing I need is the leathery trophy in my pocket.

Ear Worms
Chapter 9
The Blade

So where were we? Oh yes, the pavement rushing to meet me, at a pace faster than my mind could grasp.

SPLAT!

Unfortunately, my attempt to take a happy pedestrian with me to the other side was unsuccessful. However, I inadvertently collided with a substantial iron bollard situated at the curb.

I don't know why I jumped feet first, but I figured it wouldn't matter from this height. It turns out, it does matter. If I could go back and do it again, I would dive head first. (Well actually, if I could go back, I would have told Shane to fuck off and sit somewhere else in that classroom on the first day of school.)

Right, a little bit of warning. If you have a nervous disposition (well, first of all, you probably

Ear Worms

shouldn't have started reading my story), then it's about to get worse. I know this upcoming segment of my tale is going to be quite graphic, but I think it's important to understand what happened to me next. Don't say I didn't warn you.

When I landed, the first thing I hit was the floor with my feet. So far so good. Except, in the smallest split of a second, the next thing I had contact with was the bollard into my crotch. As my legs obliterated into a thousand pieces, the metal pillar split me in two, lengthwise. Opening me up and splitting my torso in half. Obviously, as my body was still moving into the immovable object at such speed, all my flesh and organs spilled out either side of the bollard, like some oversized play-dough toy. At the speed I was travelling, the blunt statue turned into a saw, cutting me straight down the middle.

The violent collision sent my organs hurtling to the sky, creating a gruesome spectacle reminiscent of an explosion in an abattoir, with a grotesque eruption of blood and human tissue that horrified onlookers.

Now, here's the really interesting thing that happened. My accuracy was so pin-point perfect that as my body was being carved into two equal portions, the top of the post didn't know what to do with my head, so the tip of the bollard wedged itself into my brain and just out of the top of my skull, breaking my face in two parts, but not quite all the way through, resulting in my fleshy skull, perching on the pike, for all to see, like some macabre, too realistic jack o' lantern. My flesh and bone all jellied and dressed around the gory totem pole.

The blast area must have been 20 feet wide, and parts of me could be spotted stuck to some third-story windows. At that height and speed, your body just turns into a human-sized balloon of blood.

There were a few seconds of no sound except a bus pulling away and those fucking crows

Ear Worms

still cawing somewhere in the vicinity, probably excited to pick at what was left of me. The unwilling audience to my own suicide attempt tried to comprehend what had just happened. A girl in a wheelchair picked a piece of my shin bone out of her lap. A lady who was slapped across the cheek by a slab of my thigh was trying to steady herself.

Once everybody could finally comprehended the gruesome scene, the silence ended and the screaming ensued. Scores of previously happy students' and lecturers' lives, potentially scarred by my final selfish act. Not that it bothered me, I'd been selfish all my life. What's one more moment of inconsideration?

Now, I can tell what you're thinking. How am I able to tell you all this? Unfortunately, I think you already know the answer. Apparently, when attempting to "destroy my body," this leap from 19 stories high wasn't high enough.

So how am I still alive? I wish I could answer that question. Even my brain has been

Ear Worms

mashed up inside my skull and jellied out of my nose. But I'm still here, head wedged on top of this pole.

The most eagle-eyed of onlookers of this grisly scene may have noticed that the one remaining eye in my head was moving left to right. But, alas, chaos reigned and of course nobody checked. Why would anybody think to find my pulse? I didn't even have any wrists anymore.

Now I want to ask you a question, think back to the last time you stubbed your toe, or banged your funny bone. You have that brief moment when you try to internalise the pain, but ultimately your suffering is victorious and you have to let out the scream, but after this exclamation, you feel cathartic and can continue with your day.

My agony was overwhelming (obviously), and to compound matters, I found myself incapable of finding any release for it. I wasn't even sure where my mouth was to scream, (but I'm pretty

Ear Worms

sure I saw some teeth take out the eye of aforementioned homeless man). All I had left was pain.

Of course, nobody was coming to try and save me, why would they? There wasn't anything to rescue. I had no saviour. Just what remained of my body, my pain, and my guilt.

I tried to see if I could spot Shane in the crowd but apparently, even a ghost didn't want to witness such horror.

After the screaming died down, and the crowd had dissipated, and the teams of medics and police came to cordon off the scene, I prayed that someone would look at me in the face and see the movement in my eye. One is fairly limited to how much they can move their eye, but I was blinking so much, I could feel the eyeball edging out of its socket. Of course, eventually, the eye slipped out of my head and my last lifeline to prove myself present, was gone.

I am quickly scooped into four different yellow, biological-waste bags and everything goes

Ear Worms

black again, and I'm thrown into the back of some vehicle.

It's an odd sensation, being able to feel all your body in different places, It sort of feels like I am sitting on my own head. I suppose this is what it feels like being turned inside out. I can smell my kidney next to my nose somewhere and I resent not drinking more water.

After what is left of me arrives at the hospital, I wonder what will happen to my remains. It's not like they can donate any of my body parts to anyone, I'm far too damaged. I can hear a muffled voice explaining what happens next to the 4 yellow bags. I strain to hear but it's futile. That is until one specific word stands out. I heard it correctly, and it's my only saving grace. How am I this lucky! Something has to go wrong. Maybe I misheard? No! The hospital porter said it again. There is no doubt in my mind, I am finally off to meet my maker.

The incinerator!

Ear Worms

FIRE!

Of course! After all this. I can't actually live forever, there MUST be an end, and now finally, there is a light at the end of this agonising tunnel. All my ridiculous attempts at suicide, but now I finally get my wish!

FIRE!!!

The man with the tattooed face can fuck right off! I'm getting the last laugh. Shane and I together at last. The ending is in sight. All the pain surging through my system fades away, and this feeling is so sweet.

Shane…here I come, mate.

I make an educated guess that I am being transported on some sort of trolley, and as I am being transferred to meet my maker, a bag of my meat falls off and a burst of light enters my vision. This must be the bag with my remaining eye, and the contents of said bag have spilled onto the hospital floor.

Ear Worms

"Oh for fuck's sake!" says the young hospital porter. "This is all I need."

He stands still for a few seconds contemplating how to deal with this mess.

"Come on, mate," I try to will into his consciousness, "let's go! I'm so close to the finish line!"

He checks to see if anybody is around, and seeing the coast is clear, he shuffles to the side of the trolley, and in a blink of an eye, he is out of sight.

I hear a metallic hinge open up and something clangs into place.

"What are you doing?!" I try to shout but I'm not convinced my tongue was ever collected as I can still taste wet leaves.

The bag closes up, and once again, I am blind, for the last time.

Now I am moving again but not on the trolley. It's at a much faster rate, and far smoother than the previous method of transport.

Ear Worms

THUD!

Then nothing.

Then more of nothing, for a long time. I can't tell you how long as I have no frame of reference. It could have been hours, could have been days, maybe even weeks. And it stinks.

Every foul smell made by man is here. Excrement, piss, rotten food. There is some writhing under me and something else crawls around my armpit and into my lung. I know where I am. I completely give up on the idea of the incinerator.

The cheap fucking cunt threw me down the rubbish chute.

More time passes but I don't know how long. Eventually, I'm moved and I can feel my bits of flesh crushing against myself in the back of some rubbish truck. That was pretty exciting. Occasionally, I overhear the bin men chat to each other. Mundane conversations about football and the weather. To hear voices fill me with some sort

Ear Worms

of misguided hope that I have a way out of this nightmare. False optimism corrupts my psyche a little bit more. Of course, the idle chit-chat ended as soon as it started, and that is the last voice I ever hear.

    I assume I'm in some sort of landfill now. Smells change sometimes, which is interesting. But not very often, maybe once every few years. The maggots and the worms are my friends now. Sometimes I think of Shane, but I haven't seen him since the incident at Rufus Blake tower. Somewhere deep in my mind I can still hear that damn Shakin' Stevens song. I well up when I hear it but I'm not sure where the tears are being produced. That song is my little reminder of the only time I could have saved Shane. That night in the pub. I should have gone to war on my own, and very possibly died on that battlefield. That one selfish act condemned both of us. Him to death, me to life.

Ear Worms

So here I am, for eternity I guess, still with my PTSD, unable to talk, unable to move.

During extended periods of warmth, the heat has the peculiar effect of hastening the decay of certain food items, occasionally prompting me to shift ever so slightly. That's fun. I look forward to those days.

The bugs won't eat me. Turns out maggots and worms only eat meat that is dead. I am still very much alive, defying all medical odds.

After a few years have passed, a startling realisation struck me: the ear I had taken from the Argentine soldier might be the very object responsible for the curse afflicting me. I know it's in here with me somewhere. Perhaps If I had disposed of the ear when I was able-bodied, then maybe the curse would have been lifted.

Best not to dwell on that. I think the ear is lodged somewhere in my sternum.

I guess that's it.

Ear Worms
THE ~~END~~ BEGINNING.

ACKNOWLEDGEMENTS

Massive shout out to Spike Z Stephenson for making this wicked cover art. The dude really understood the creative direction is was aiming for, go check him out on Instagram @spike_zephaniah

Also I'd like to thank mum and sister for proof reading and helping my tangled web of dyslexic words become legible. Cheers Diane and Bella!

Lastly, shoutout to my remaining cat Leatherface for always catching our dinner.

Printed in Great Britain
by Amazon